Ted Allan in

an histori

Norman Allan

the skinny: …

January 1937: Ted Allan turned 21 and readied to travel to Madrid to report on the Civil War for the Daily Clarion, the Canadian communist newspaper, and to work with his mentor, Norman Bethune - but Fred Rose, the Party Leader, has neglected to tell the Clarion...

To get to Madrid was an imperative. Ted Allan enlisted in the International Brigade; traveling to Spain with 26 other North American volunteers... The Brigade sends Ted to Madrid to report... on Bethune! We learn that all 26 of Ted's traveling companions were dead within six weeks..

Ted tangled with a bitter, and envious, Ernest Hemingway. (He had been kissing the bride to be.)

Ted meets with Robert Capa, the war photographer, and his companion, Gerda Taro. In the movie, when Ted is troubled about how to handle "the problem with Bethune", Gerda suggests to Ted that he send Bethune to China.* Ted sends Beth back to Canada, and on ?

Capa leaves Gerda in Ted's "care". Of course Ted falls in love. Ted and Gerda visit the front to report on the battle of Brunette

Will the cub reporter from Canada and the lovely war photographer survive the battle of Bruenette... ?

* in the book, ",,,: the movie," we will learn that this is not true is just a fiction of the movie... a Hollywood plot**
** subplot? piece of shtick I think it is quite cute

an historical novel by

Norman Allan

Ted Allan in Spain:
the movie

a graphic novel
first draft

self-published POD
by Norman Allan
on **create**space

ISBN-13: 978-1511437721 (CreateSpace-Assigned)
ISBN-10: 1511437723
BISAC: Fiction / Historical

first published on the 26th March 2015 on CreateSpace

note: this is the first (official) edition of
Ted Allan in Spain: the movie
by Norman Allan
April 2015

self-published POD
by Norman Allan

on **create**space
Title ID: 5394914

Heart of the heartless world,
Dear heart, the thought of you
Is the pain at my side,
The shadow that chills my view.
The wind rises in the evening,
Reminds that autumn is near.
I am afraid to lose you,
I am afraid of my fear.
On the last mile to Huesca,
The last fence for our pride,
Think so kindly, dear, that I
Sense you at my side.
And if bad luck should lay my strength
Into the shallow grave,
Remember all the good you can;
Don't forget my love.

John Cornford

preface:

Actually, this book, *Ted Allan in Spain: the movie,* is an historical novel. But, I want you to think of it as a film, as a movie, so we'll start in script form. (Note: every pair of even and odd, facing, pages might have a cell of a "story board".) And we might boast of our movie stars…

starring   Ernest Hemingway
                  Norman Bethune
                  Robert Capa
                  Gerda Taro

and introducing… Marlon Brando as Ted Allan

also note that here we are publishing just the text, and that many illustrations associated with this text are available, for free, at

http://www.normanallan.com/Lit/TAiS/TAiS%20illustrations.htm

The first draft runs thus…

Ted Allan in Spain: the movie

by

Norman Allan

Norman Allan
555 Raven Rd.
Toronto Ont.

OVER A DARK SCREEN:

> NORMAN (V.O.)
> Ted, tell us about your time in Spain,
> in the Civil War.

FADE IN:

INT. NEWSROOM OF THE DAILY CLARION - DAY

An ASSISTANT leads TED through a small newspaper
news-room. (And perhaps this is in black and white
to put us in a 1937 frame of reference.)

> NARRATOR (V.O.)
> Originally, I thought I was going to go
> as the Daily Clarion's war
> correspondent. The Clarion was Canada's
> communist newspaper. January 1937. I
> went up to Toronto to pick up my
> credentials."

Ted Allan (the ideal casting would be a young
Marlon Brando, with an Anglophone Montreal
accent)… Ted is shown into the editor's office.
Leslie Morris, the Editor, rises to greet him

> EDITOR
> Ted Allan, cub reporter… Sorry, our
> rising star Montreal reporter. Great to
> see you. What brings you to Toronto?"

> TED
> And now special war correspondent, I
> thought. I thought I should talk with
> you before taking off.

> EDITOR
> (shrugs.)
> War correspondent? I don't understand.

                    TED
          I'm going to Spain.
                    (he pats his pocket)
          Passport. Ticket. Sailing next week.
          I've been planning this with the Party,
          with Fred, Fred Rose. He told me,
          several times, that he'd talked to you.

                    EDITOR
          Fred Rose, The Party Chairman, that is,
          mentioned the possibility. "Ted might,"
          he said. He seemed to be just floating
          a balloon. He did not say, "Leslie, Ted
          is going. The Party wants you to send
          Ted Allan. He just speculated. And, if
          you had arrived here yesterday morning,
          I'd have said, "Fine," and you could
          have gone as the Clarion's correspond-
          dent, but yesterday Jean Watts, from
          New York, came in and offered to
          dispatch to us from Spain. So now she's
          our Madrid correspondent."

                    TED
                    (in disbelief)
          I checked this, I double checked this
          with Fred three, four time over the
          last weeks. He said he'd talked to you.

                    EDITOR
          That's our chairman.
                    (Leslie Morris shrugs again),

DISSOLVE TO

INT. COMMUNIST PARTIES HEADQUARTERS, MONTREAL -
DAY

TED ALLAN and FRED ROSE are standing facing each
other in Fred Rose's office, Ted talking with
passion.

                    TED
You said you'd spoken to him.

                    FRED
I spoke to him a while ago. I told him
you wanted to go.

                    TED
I've got my passport, ticket, said my
goodbyes.

                    FRED
The Party needs you here in Montreal.

                    TED
I'm going to Spain.

                    FRED
The Party wants you here in Montreal.

                    TED
I'll join in the International Brigade.

                    FRED
You'd die in the trenches.

                    TED
I'm going to Spain. I'll enlist.

                    FRED
If you insist, you will die in the
trenches.

DISSOLVE TO MONTAGE: two old trucks crossing the
Pyrenees.

ROLL CREDITS: *"Ted Allan in Spain"*

                    NARRATOR   (V.O.)
          We came over the mountains, into
          Spain, on the backs of two old
          trucks. Twenty young Americans,
          seven Canadians, new recruits to
          fight fascism.

CREDITS: *Starring Ernest Hemingway*

                    NARRATOR   (V.O.)
          Wrapped in blankets: January
          25th,1937. Cold enough. My twenty
          first birthday. Me, I'm Ted Allan.
          A volunteer. Spirits high, but
          scared: Life on the line.

CREDITS: *Dr. Norman Bethune.*

                    NARRATOR   (V.O.)
          Sure. Like Fred said, we were all
          probably going die, but the
          fascists, the Nazis had to be
          stopped, whatever the cost.

CREDITS: *Robert Capa*

MONTAGE: flatbed at the back of a truck with about
a dozen young men hunkered together. And one
woman, Jean Watts, the reporter now for the Daily
Clarion in Spain. We hear the trucks engine
laboring as it climbs the mountains.

                    NARRATOR   (V.O.)

          The trucks groaning round hair-
          pins. Night falling. Sleeping out
          in the open. Shivering till sleep.

CREDITS: *and Gerda Taro*

                    NARRATOR   (V.O.)
          Then cross rolling lands and
          plains. Couldn't see much from the
          back of the trucks. Finally to
          Albacete, the staging centre for
          the International Brigade.
          Billeted on the floor of a large
          room, hall, they called it a
          barracks. An old factory? In the
          night the planes came. German? The
          bombs fell."

SOUND: cacophony of bombs exploding.

CREDITS: *and introducing: Ted Allan*

MONTAGE: the volunteers, TED included, digging in
the smoldering ruins of the bombed apartments of
Albacete.

                    NARRATOR (CONT'D V.O.)
          We joined the rescue teams.
          Digging through ruins. I helped
          unburied a child, a boy, maybe
          four years old. Still warm, but
          broken, still, lifeless.

MONTAGE: TED cradling a dead child.

                    NARRATOR (CONT'D V.O.)
          I'll write about this," I heard my
          self say. "Don't be a creep, a
          phony!" I chided myself, but I
          already had a title: *"This Time a
          Better Earth"*.
               Did I sleep on the hard
          floor a few hours near dawn?
          Maybe.

DISSOLVE TO: ALBACETE, BULLRING - DAY

Two hundred young men stand in a ragged line, in
the empty arena. They are being inducted into the
International Brigade. They are already in
uniform.

COLONEL KERRIGAN, with HIS ATTACHÉ, is reviewing
them, interviewing them one by one.

                    NARRATOR   (V.O.)
               Any of us who could drive a truck
               or ride a motor-cycle got assigned
               to transport or communications.
               The rest of us were canon fodder."

Kerrigan is addressing JIM LENTHIER who is next to
TED
                    KERRIGAN
               And what were you doing back
               home?"
                    LENTHIER
               I ran a theatre company. I'm an
               actor. A director.

                    KERRIGAN
               That's wonderful. Perhaps when
               things quiet down, you can
               organize some entertainment for
               us. We'll try to keep in touch.

Kerrigan moves on to face the next recruit. Ted.

                    NARRATOR
               Kerrigan probably thought to
               himself, how quickly they die
               here, our artists, our writers, as
               he turned from John to me.

                    KERRIGAN
               Your name?

                    TED
          Ted Allan.

                    KERRIGAN
          And what were you doing before you
          came over?

                    TED
          I was a reporter. With the Daily
          Clarion, in Montreal.

                    KERRIGAN
                    (frowns)
          We've lost so many writers.
          Cornford, Fox. Do you know their
          work?

Ted nods and pulls a slim book from his back
pocket. He shows the book to Kerrigan while he,
Ted, recites.

                    TED
          "AND IF BAD LUCK SHOULD LAY MY
          STRENGTH INTO THE SHALLOW GRAVE;
          REMEMBER ALL THE GOOD YOU CAN…"
          Cornford,[i] of course. It's as
          though he knew. I guess we do.

                    KERRIGAN
                    (pauses to think)
          I think I'm going send you to
          Madrid to report to, to report for
          the Brigade there."

                    TED
          But my comrades…

                    KERRIGAN
          Your objection is duly noted. And
          commended. Report to the officer's
          mess. We'll sort you out there
          later.

Kerrigan moves on to the next volunteer in the line.

DISSOLVE TO: THE OFFICERS MESS - EVENING

Ted is sitting at a table writing notes. Kerrigan comes in with GEORGE MARION. They join Ted.

                    KERRIGAN
          Ted Allan. This is George Marion,
          a reporter for the London Daily
          Worker. Ted's from Montreal, Wrote
          for the… What's it called?

                    TED
          The Daily Clarion, but I'm not
          their correspondent here. I've got
          credentials with the Federated
          Press, the union news-service.
          Small fry.

                    MARRION
          You're from Montreal. Do you know
          Doctor Bethune?

                    TED
          Yes, of course. Actually, I was
          going to go and work with him and
          the Blood Transfusion Unit, when I
          thought I was coming over for the
          Clarion. I know him well.

                    MARRION
          There are disturbing rumors coming
          out the Unit. They say that's a
          Civil War in itself, as good as.

                    KERRIGAN
          What sort of rumors?

                    MARRION
          Any number. Bethune fights with
          the Spanish doctors. Bethune
          drinks.

                    KERRIGAN
                    (to Ted)
          So perhaps you can go to Bethune's
          Unit and report on it, report on
          it to the Brigade; report on the
          situation to Comrade Gallo in
          Madrid. Can you do that?

TED nods. Mouths yes.

                    TED
          May I also report to Bethune and
          to the Canadian Party?

                    KERRIGAN
          If you wish, perhaps. Speak to
          Comrade Gallo about that.
                    (to his attaché)
          Write out a pass to Madrid for Ted
          Allan.

INT. CAB OF A TRUCK ON THE ROAD TO MADRID - NIGHT

Driving through the night with no lights. Ted in
the cab with the driver.

                    NARRATOR (V.O.)
          I came by truck, again, from
          Albacete. This time in the cab.
          Arrived in Madrid exhausted.

INT. BLOOD TRANSFUSION UNIT, AN OFFICE - DAY

BETHUNE and TED

                    NARRATOR (V.O.)
          The Blood Transfusion Unit was
          housed in a recently abandoned
          mansion in a wealth Madrid suburb,
          a neighborhood untouched by the
          war. A palatial mansion with its
          own grounds. The fascist didn't
          shell their own abandoned houses.
                    Beth greeted me warmly,
          hugging me, embracing me, laughing
          at the way I looked in my
          International Brigade uniform.

BETH indicates to TED to turn round, to spin
round, which he does.

                    NARRATOR (V.O.) (CONT'D)
          I couldn't stop my sudden weeping.
          With in minutes he had me sitting
          at a huge dinning table: coffee,
          rolls, and terrible tasting
          margarine!

                    BETHUNE
          So how come you're in uniform and
          not here for the Clarion?

                    TED
          Fred forgot to phone Toronto to
          tell them.

                    BETHUNE
          Our infallible leader. But in that
          case, why aren't you at the front?

                    TED
          When I mentioned I was a reporter.
                    (pauses)

                    TED (CONT'D)
        It's a long story, Beth. The
        Brigade wants me to find out
        what's happening here, in the
        Unit. They've sent me to report,
        and I guess that means assess
        what's happening in some way.

                    BETHUNE
        To spy!

Ted nods, smiles - a boyish, totally open grin.

                    BETHUNE (CONT'D)
        Well someone should find out
        what's going on here. That's it!
        I'm going to make you commissar,
        political officer, for the Unit.
        You find out what's going on here
        and report to the Brigade, to the
        Party, and to me, face to face.
             I personally think that
        Doctors Culebras and Gonzalez, the
        Spanish doctors with the Unit, are
        fascist sympathizers. I think they
        are trying to sabotage the Unit.
        But you'll find out.
             Political officer, Commissar.
        I think the rank of Colonel might
        go with that. But enough. Let me
        show you your room. You'll stay
        with us here, of course. And I'll
        introduce you to the team. Here,
        bring your duffle bag."

FADEOUT

I am going to move from a script format to a prose format. I think that it is easier to read, but remember, I'm still describing "*Ted Allan in Spain: the movie.*"

We fade in on a government office where Ted is meeting with comrade Gallo. Indeed, the narrator tells us: "Next day I met with Comrade Gallo. Gallo was the *nom de guerre* of Luigi Longo, one of the leaders of the International Brigade. From Italy, the illegal Italian party. He had help set it up the Brigade and now bore the title of Inspector General. We exchanged pleasantries, and I briefed him, very briefly, on the Bethune, Blood Transfusion Unit issues."

Ted tells Gallo, "There isn't much I can report yet. The Unit is geared up top deliver blood at the front. They've been doing that. But Bethune is a free spirit. Beth thinks that the Spanish doctors are collaborators, saboteurs."

Gallo speaks fluent English, but with an Italian accent. "Comrade Bethune is doing great work for the cause here in Spain. But war is difficult for everyone. A little drinking, a little tension, a little paranoia, is to be expected. You watch, Observe. Be his friend. *Sul serio.* I mean that sincerely. Keep us posted. Take your time."

"There another matter I'd like to discuss," says Ted. "I'm wondering if it would be possible for me to broadcast, report on radio from Madrid to North America."

"That would be for Spanish government, for Constancia de la Mora, to decide. She's head of the government's press bureau. We will have to send you to Valencia to talk with her about that. First find your feet here in Madrid. Find out what's going on with the city, with the war... with Bethune."

Ted, "And I wanted to ask about my status, my rank, my roll in the Brigade."

"You'll report to me. You needn't wear uniform. You'll be a reporter." Gallo consults his notes. "You have your Federated Press credentials. File your stories, your dispatches with them. And you will be a medical worker, volunteer with Bethune. Dress for your work. If you are his political officer, that would be a matter for the Canadian Party. Nothing to do with the Brigade. For the Brigade you will aid Bethune, and report. Serve the people."

Ted returns to the Blood Transfusion Unit. There is a lot of commotion, bustle around, people busy, scurrying round. Among these we might recognize Jean Watts.

Bethune notices Ted and shouts, "There you are. There's a battle on the Jarama, just east of the city. We'll be going first thing in the morning. You've met Henning Sise?" He indicates a tall, patrician-like, young man. Henning, a Finnish-Canadian, has been working with Beth from the start. Standing next to him is a gorgeous, tall, blond woman. Bethune continues his introductions, "And Ingrid. Ingrid, this is Ted."

Henning excuses himself, lifts a box from the table, and walks off.

And Beth continues. "Ingrid's a reporter from Stockholm with the *Svenska Dagblatet.*" He accentuates the words in an attempt at a Swedish accent, and repeats, "*Svenska Dagblatet.* She's doing an interview with me on the Unit."

"An in depth interview," says Ingrid. She has a sunshine rainbow smile. And she winks.

"Dr. Culebras' sister is scandalized that Ingrid's sharing my room," Beth points. In the background we see a middle-aged nun carrying a box through the office. "But I too am catholic, and I say that it is good for my morale!" There is a sound of breaking glass and commotion in the other room. "Wait a moment," say Beth, hurrying towards the door. Ted and Ingrid follow.

In the other room, Dr Culebras has been packing a crate with bottles blood and has dropped one, broken on the floor, blood everywhere.

"Idiot." shouts Bethune.

There is a shocked silence.

"Yes, an idiot is a dolt in any language, but," says Bethune, addressing Culebras, "you're either a fool or a spy, and I'm giving you the benefit of the doubt."

Culebras retorts indignantly in Spanish. The sister glares at Beth. Bethune chastises her too. "Hungry people gave their precious blood for their sons, for their brothers at the front. Sloppy, fat, well fed people are spilling it." Beth huffs, puffs, and turns and walks away. He turns back to Ted and says softly over his shoulder, "Ted, come with me. I want to show you something."

They walk to Ted's room. There is a portable typewriter on the table by the bed.

Beth: "I noticed you writing long-hand, and that you didn't have a type writer. That's was fine when you were going to the trenches." He pauses a beat. "But a writer needs a typewriter."

Ted, jaw-dropped, looks at the typewriter.

"You need it more than I do," says Beth. "We've got three typewriters in the office."

"Oh, Beth." Ted is breathless.

The narrator, voice over: "Sometimes Beth was like a father to me. And sometimes he drank."

Beth and Ted walk back to the offices. Bethune pours himself a large shot from a liqueur bottle. He indicates for Ted to help himself. Beth walks towards the room with the spilt blood. Looks in. Ingrid and Henning are mopping up the broken glass and blood.

Bethune raises his voice. "You shouldn't be doing that!" Then he bellows. "Culebras! Come and clean up your mess!"

Ingrid and Henning continue their cleaning. Bethune turns to leave the room. Slams the door behind him.

Cut to: the road to Jarama. Ted, Bethune, and Henning squashed in the front of one of the Unit's ambulances – a modified station wagon with a large, loud refrigeration unit in the back. They've been driving through the countryside outside Madrid. Prosaic and idyllic. Quiet and peaceful. Ted, though, is anxious. Bethune chatters, talks of bringing the ambulances into Spain.

"So Henning, here, and I drove the two ambulances down from London in November, was it? They sailed over the Pyrenees. And they're doing the job."

Ted: "Beth, you're sure you know where we're going?"
Bethune: "Relax."

Two bullets shatter the windscreen just over Bethune and Ted's heads. Ted dives for the floor of the ambulance. Bethune gently, serenely, brings the vehicle to a stop. Henning opens the door before they have fully stopped. He jumps out and dives into the ditch beside the road. Ted scrambles to follow, tumbling into the ditch on top of Henning.

Throughout all this a machine gun is continuing to chatter. Henning is pale and shaking. Ted is giggling anxiously, on the border of hysteria.

Coming up the road, in the distance, an Italian tank is bearing down on them.

Meanwhile Bethune has walks nonchalantly, no heed of the gunfire, round to the back of the ambulance and opens the back doors. He shouts with spirit and some distain, "Get on up out of that ditch. We've got four cases of blood in the back here. Get them out."

Ted and Henning climb reluctantly, hesitantly, from the ditch. Cowering, they help Bethune remove the four cases and place them in the ditch. Bullets whiz round them, at least Ted sure thinks they do. Bethune is calm and unperturbed.

The tank continues to advance towards the three Canadians now sheltering in the ditch.

Ted: "Shit! We're going to be massacred."

Bethune: "Not necessarily."

We see a close up of Ted's face showing surprise.

Bethune continues, "They'll see our medical insignias, the *Socorro Rojo*, Red Cross, and just take us prisoner."

Ted turns to Henning and asks sarcastically, "Is optimism useful or crazy in war?"

There is a tense wait as the Italian tank continues to approach. And then from out of nowhere, a Republican tank appears, and another, and a third, and the Italian tank turns and trundles, at a pace, away.

"Without optimism," says Bethune, "people are hopeless. Lost"

I want to establish a dialogue between the narrator and a second voice, which might be mine, talking to Ted (Ted the narrator). This second voice over is the author's voice, Norman Allan, I'm Ted Allan's son. Can I get away with this, this new voice? Ted would say, "Just try it. Write it. Get it out. Get it down anyhow. It doesn't have to be perfect. You can always edit."

The problem here, the reason for this "aside", is that I can't envisage the field hospital, the medical unit at the front. (And we don't have the budget yet, in our film project, to hire researchers. And also I may to need this devise later. We'll see…)

The field hospital is a hive of activity. The sounds of war are in the background. They are present, but muffled. For me, the author (not the narrator), the closest I've been to this scene are visits to first world hospitals, and scenes from the movie MASH, but the field hospital is not modern, and there is no humour. Bustle and pain. Hurry, scurry, wait.

Bethune, assisted by Henning, is focused on delivering blood transfusions to those in need. They've triaged. Now they are setting up the apparatus. We watch as Bethune inserts a hypodermic-needle into the arm of a young soldier who is missing a leg. A bloody bandage. Moaning softly, muttering, "madre mi madre." (That's Ted's dialogue, so I'm betting it's authentic.)

We watch Bethune comforting the young soldier, who is perhaps eighteen years old, a teen. Bethune: "*¿tu nombre.*" (SUBTITLES: Your name?)

Soldier, "*Soy Juan.*" He's gritting his teeth from the pain. "Madre mi madre."

Bethune, touching the young soldier's shoulder tenderly: "*Vas a estar bien.*" (SUBTITLES: You are going to be fine.) Bethune offers the youth, the teen, a cigarette. Lights it for him.

Ted asks Bethune, "What can I do?"

Bethune, "How's your Spanish?"

Ted shrugs, "There wasn't much time."

Beth, "Crash course now, eh."

A Spanish doctor is walking passed them. Beth asks, "*Por favor. ¿Qué puede hacer mi amigo para ayudar.*" (SUBTITLES: Please, how can my friend be of help?)

Spanish Doctor, "*Si pudiera hablar español, podria cambiar los orinales.*" (SUBTITLE: If he could speak Spanish, he could change the bedpans.)

Beth shrugs. He doesn't understand. To Ted he says, "We'll train you later. For now, just watch." Beth continues, "This child here," indicting the youth he has just been smoking with, "he was in shock. Now he's alert. Blood saves lives."

Ted goes to a corner where he's out of the way. He sits. He, and we, watch activity in the Field Hospital. He takes out a notebook and writes a short note. He looks up again, observing a long, long time.

The film dissolves to show the passage of time and fades back in to the field hospital at night, dim and quiet. Early morning. Ted, still in his chair, is waking. The narrator tells us, "I woke at 4 in the morning. Everything quiet, still, except there's Beth working, setting up another transfusion for an ailing, possibly dying, soldier.

We watch Beth changing the bottle, and then sitting beside the young soldier, again hand on the shoulder. Then Bethune reaches into his shirt pocket, pulls out a small vial, opens the vial, pours out a small pill into the cap of the vial, offers it to and pours it into the young soldier's mouth.

Beth notices Ted awake. and says, "They are children. Just children." He looks at his patient. "I wonder what are his dreams?"

"What was that you just gave him?" Ted asks.

"Oh," says Beth. "There is this French doctor with the Brigade, a Dr. Jacque Benveniste. He gives all his trauma patients, it's called *Arnica*. And his patients are doing remarkably better than anyone else's. It's called homeopathy. Some sort of magic."

"I've heard of that," says Ted. "It's not scientific."

"Ah," says Bethune, "but you've got to remember Bethune's Law of Effective Medical Practice."

"Which is?" prompts Ted.

"If it works, use it!"

"Pragmatism," says Ted.

"Indeed," says Beth." Empiricism." Then he adds, "And remember, Pasteur's invisible germinators of disease weren't scientific until Koch discovered the Tuberculosis bacillus."

"Here," says Beth. "I've got a spare vial. You should carry this with you." He hand Ted the vial. "You never know when you'll meet trauma in a war zone, but you can count on it."

Then we watch the still night. Bethune comforting the wounded. And the NARRATOR (V.O) tells us, "Over a period of weeks I learned to assist in the transfusion unit. Oh, and I started writing dispatches for the Federated Press, and I met with the press, other reporters, photographers."

Dissolve to a Montage of a 1930s car driving along a Spanish highway.

NARRATOR (CONT'D V.O.), "I met with the journalist community in Madrid, and with the local censor, Arturo Barea. Met again with Comrade Gallo. We discussed my broadcasting project, and Gallo sent me to Valencia to talk about it to the Republican Government.

Interior of an office the Republican government in Valencia. Ted is talking with Constancia de la Mora, a handsome, middle aged woman. They are talking with enthusiasm, though to being with, we are listening to the Narrators voice.

Narrator: "Constancia de la Mora was in charge of the government press bureau. An incredible woman. A novelist. We got on famously. We arranged that I'd broadcast once a week, in the middle of the night, 2 in the morning, to the Americas from the government radio station in Madrid."

We start to listen to their conversation. Constancia is saying, "So you'll go to the Telefonica Building in Madrid and meet with senor Gonzalez, the Station Manager. He'll make all the arrangements for you. You are going back to Madrid tomorrow?"

Ted: "In the morning."

Constancia: "Then there is a small favour I would ask. There is a correspondent, for Collier's Magazine, looking for a ride to Madrid."

Ted makes a face.

Constancia (continues): "You will not be sorry when you see her."

Ted: "In that case by all means."

Constancia: "There is a man, an acquaintance of her's, to travel too."

Ted: "C'est la guerre."

EXTERIOR: THE ENTRANCE OF THE HOTEL VICTORIA IN VALENCIA, MORNING. Martha Gellhorn, an attractive young, blond, woman in her mid to late twenties, is standing by the entrance. Constancia de la Mora and Ted pull up, and step out of the government car that Ted has been assigned. Constancia waves, and Martha Gellhorn descends the steps to join them. Martha is dressed in casual, but expensive, clothes. Her manner is cultured, refined.

Constancia introduce Ted to Martha. She explains that Martha is a journalist and a novelist. "Her novel," Constancia tells Ted, ""The Trouble I've Seen", is excellent. Wonderful." She continues, "Martha has only just arrived in Spain and doesn't know much about the situation here, so I'd be very grateful to you if you would brief her on policy matters."

Ted: "I'll be glad to."

A taxi pulls up. The driver steps out and opens the rear door. Sidney Franklin emerges. A dignified, though possibly affected, bearing. He settles the fare with the driver, and turns towards the hotel entrance. Constancia waves to him and beckons him. "Sidney, this is Ted Allan, a journalist with the Brigade, and the Senor who will give you a lift to Madrid. Ted, this is Sidney Franklin, the famous "Matador from Brooklyn"."

"Ole!" says Ted. "Our Jewish toreador." Sidney waves off the comment away. Ted continues, "Did you know that over half the volunteers with the Brigade are Jewish?"

Sidney ignores him. Says, "I'll put my bag in the boot."

Ted (to Martha), "Well, if I'm going to brief you, Martha, we'd best sit together in the back." He opens the door for her. Walks round to the passenger's side. Opens the front door. "Mr. Franklin, your seat."

INT: CAR ON THE ROAD TO MADRID, DAY
Ted and Martha Gellhorn sit in the back seat of the car, with space between them, as they leave Valencia. Ted speaks of Spain's recent history. Lectures. Martha listens, a little smile on her face. "Let's see," Ted begins, "the Second Republic was founded a few years back in 1931, and Spain continues split between a right wing, the National Front and a left wing Popular Front. Very unstable. Lots of tensions, civil strife. Back and forth. In last February's general election,1936, the Popular Front won. A narrow victory." Ted holds his thumb and index finger close together. The camera pans to the front of the car, the driver intent on the road as they leave the city. Honks at a farmer and his son driving cattle along the road. The camera pans to Franklin, looking suspiciously over his shoulder. We dissolve to a long shot of the car driving through the countryside. We hear Ted, continuing voice over. "Then in the summer, last July, a part, a section of the army, "the four insurgent generals", revolted. Generalissimo Franco invaded with the colonial army from Morocco…"

FADE TO: Ted and Martha in the back seat. Martha's now closer. Their hips, thighs, touch. Martha places a hand on Ted's knee. Ted continues the "briefing". "So Spain, and the army, are divided in two. The Loyalists, the Republican government, Popular front, hold the industrial heart of the country, and Catalonia and the Basque region. The fascists, the Nationalist, hold much of the country side, most of the food production."

FADE TO: Martha is cuddled up against. Ted has put his arm around her. "The core of the Nationalist army are the battle hardened African corps, and at first their advance was irresistible. Last November they were at the gates of Madrid. They crossed the Manzanares river, advanced into the University Campus, but there, in hand-to-hand fighting, we held them. Half a mile, a mile, from the center of Madrid."

We dissolve to a long shot of the car driving through the countryside. Again we hear Ted's voice over. "Then there is the situation with the Non-Intervention Pact, where England and France have the Republic virtually blockaded. Meanwhile Mussolini and Hitler are pouring arms in to the Nationalist, the fascists. There are probably fifty to sixty thousand Italian troops, regular army, fighting with Franco, fighting for the fascist; maybe twenty thousand Germans. The only country trading with the Loyalists, with the government, is Mexico. Oh, and unofficially arms are coming from the Soviet Union."

We dissolve back into the car. Ted has stopped talking. Martha is snuggled up against him. He leans over to kiss her. The kiss soon becomes quite passionate. And it goes on. And on.

Sidney Franklin observes, angrily.

And we now listen to the narrator's voice over, telling us what we have just seen, and are watching. "Martha and I felt very comfortable together, hit it off immediately, and soon found ourselves almost sitting in each other laps, giggling and cuddling for warmth. It was a long journey. Martha and I spent nearly the whole trip kissing and necking. Almost making out."

We watch the car entering the suburbs of Madrid. Republican soldiers walking along the side of the road. And the narration continues: " When we got to Madrid I had to go to the Blood Transfusion Unit: she had to go to the Hotel Florida. I asked, "When will I see you?" She said, "Whenever you want." I said, "In a couple of hours." She said, "Fine." "

INT: A CORRIDOR IN THE HOTEL FLORIDA. MADRID. DAY
The hotel had some pretension of grandiose and elegance, but hardships of recent times shows in aging carpets and wallpaper. TED knocks on a door. "Come in," MARTHA calls (V.O.). Ted enters.

A well appointed room, though again aging. Martha, young as sunshine, sits on one side of the double bed, pats the other side for Ted to sit. Ted is carrying yellow paper carbon copies of a couple of his short stories. He sits, hands them to Martha. She places them on the bedside table. She sits there. She smiles.

Ted is hesitant. After several awkward moments he asks, "Have you got the key to the door."

Martha just sits there smiling and mouths a quiet, "No."

"For Christ's sake," says Ted. "I know you have the key. I want to lock the door."

Martha shakes her head. Continues smiling. They sit. A puzzled look on Ted's face.

Then there's a knock at the door. It opens, and a large man enters. He looks how you might imagine Hemingway. He has a latch key in his hand. He slides into a pocket. He looks mildly surprised, and then irritated.

"Oh, Come in, Hon," says Martha. "This is uh, Ted Allan. Ted, this my betrothed, Ernesto."

Ted looks at Martha. Hemingway glares at Ted. And Martha says, "I'll see you later, okay Ted?"

"Okay yeah," says the youth, getting up and leaving.

EXT: MONTAGE TED walking in the streets of Madrid. DAY.

> NARRATOR
> Decades later I read in Kert's "Hemingway's Women" an account of Martha's first days in Madrid : "After her arrival in Madrid, Ernest tried to take charge of Martha. On her very first[1] night, during a heavy bombardment, she woke up and, seeking company, found her door locked from the outside. She banged and shouted but to no avail. Finally, when the shelling stopped a hotel employee unlocked the door. Who had locked it, she wondered. She located Ernest in someone's room playing poker. He had locked it, he admitted sheepishly, so that no man could bother her."
> And later I learned that Sidney Franklin, the matador, was a close friend and associate of Hemingway's. And he had told Hemingway about Martha and me necking in the car.

---

[1] "On her second night in Madrid," Kert wrote. But this is a movie, not a documentary.

FADE TO: INT: RESTAURANT ON THE GRAND VIA. DAY Long Shot of an extended table. ARTURO BAREA sits at the head of the table. The city's foreign correspondents are assembling at the table, a handful already sitting, including TED at the far end of the table, and HEMINGWAR and GELLHORN near Barea at the head of the table.

NARRATOR: "All the correspondents used to eat in a restaurant in the Hotel Gran Via, lunch, not dinner, but lunch. The head censor in Madrid was a man called Arturo Barea. Once a week Barea would meet with the foreign correspondents. He would sometimes refer to various dispatches he thought were special or important and everyone would be very excited."

LONG SHOT of Ted meeting Capa and Gerda.:

Ted notices two new arrivals making their way over towards the journalist's table - an attractive young man and woman. Ted jumps up and hurries over to meet, to greet them. "It is an awing, an honor, it's swell,." Ted splutters. "Your work... I'm speechless."

Capa smiles.

Gerda's expression shows that she is perhaps amused, perhaps intrigued. She's interested.

Ted continues to gush, "Robert Capa! Gerda Taro!" And then, a little more composed, he continues, "I'm Ted Allan. (pause a beat) I'm going to be broadcasting, on the government radio transmitter, to America, and Canada. Starting next week. I'm going to be interviewing Bethune that first week. But the week after. If you will excuse me saying so, you two are probably not only the most famous photographers in Spain. You are probably the most famous photographers on the planet, at the moment. Can I interview you?"

"Of course," says Capa. Capa is Hungarian. He speaks with a heavy middle European accent that caresses his words. He is Jewish. He is handsome, a cultured man in his early twenties. A man of action: The original War Photographer.

Gerda Taro is German, Jewish, again a cultured, handsome person in her mid twenties. She gives a little oblique nod of her head and looks Ted in the eye; an inquiring look, which goes no further at this time as Arturo Barea taps the table with his wine glass, and everybody hurries to take their seats.

Barea begins: "I'm going to read you one of the most vivid, the most exciting dispatch I have ever read." He adjusts his glasses and the papers in front of him. Even before he starts everyone automatically turns towards Hemingway. Looks of awe. Quite dumbstruck. We are sitting in the presence of history.

> BAREA
> (reading from the yellow double spaced pages of a dispatch)
> In the night, the planes came. German Heinkels. They bombed us from midnight till dawn. They came at intervals in relays of eight, dropped their bombs, and returned, and returned. Some comrades with rifles shot skyward, but our guns were useless. There was no defense. There was nothing we could do but listen and tremble.

HEMINGWAY'S eyebrows rising in surprise, consternation. He senses that it's Ted Allan's dispatch

> BAREA (CONT'D)
> I trembled. Terror-bombing is effective. The barracks were hit, and some recruits were hurt, but miraculously no one was killed. Albacete itself, though, was bombed to ruin.

> BAREA (CONT'D)
> Most of us, the volunteers, went into the city
> to help with the rescue. Picks and shovels
> were placed in our trembling hands.

TED too is stunned, looking at all this, taking in all the awed eyes on

HEMINGWAY, and Papa Hemingway's displeasure, his glances

over at Ted.

> BAREA (CONT'D)
> All night we dug in the ruins trying to save
> those entombed in their crushed houses. I
> helped dig out the body of a child: a boy
> perhaps four years old, his bloodied head
> indented. One arm twisted at a weird angle,
> shattered bone showing through, the blood
> still oozing. I hugged the broken body close
> and sobbed.

GERDA observes Ted, Hemingway. She smiles, knowingly.

> BAREA (CONT'D)
> Newly massacred bodies emit strange and
> foul odors. There is nothing noble here. I felt I
> was in a nightmare, a dream, far away. The
> night seemed endless. Morning brought the
> relief of no more planes, no more bombs. I
> think we were all in shock. And exhausted.
> My comrades and I had worked side by side
> through the whole night barely uttering a
> word.

BACK TO THE WIDE SHOT: Barea and the foreign correspondents.

> BAREA (CONT'D)
> We returned to the barracks. One of the walls
> and part of the roof had disappeared. The
> floor we had slept on was cratered. We were
> slightly crazed and we giggled at the sight.
> Throughout the morning the air-raid sirens

BAREA (CONT'D)
moaned, but the skies were clear, a paled
blue sky washed out by the sun. The
ambulances screamed. And we dozed, and
woke, and waited.

As Barea finishes, many of the assembled jump up and gather
round Papa Hemingway. There is a buzz. Everyone looking at Papa
H. "Oh, fantastic," says one. "Great!" says another. Hemingway is
trying to wave off the compliments. "No, no!"

Ted sits circumspectly. He mumbles under his breath, "Holy
shit."

"I did not write that!" shouts an annoyed Hemingway.

"No, no!" says Barea. "Ted Allan."

Slowly the crowd turns, gawks at Ted a moment. Then there
are few cursory "very good"s and "well done"s. Then the gathering
settles back into its customary meeting mode.

DISSOLVE TO:

The gathering rising. Some wonder off. Some talk, schmooze. Ted
hurries over to Capa and Gerda. He is quite intensely focused on
Capa. "I wonder if you've time to take coffee? There is so much I
want to ask you."

Capa takes Ted's elbow. "Yes, and let's just move out front
to the terrace."

We follow Capa, Taro, Allan out to the front of the hotel.
They find a table. Order coffee.

Ted gushes to Capa: "I feel like I've known you the longest
time, yet I've never met anyone like you. Except maybe Beth."

Gerda remarks to Ted: "You've fallen in love." Gerda has a soft German accent.

"Oh, I won't chase your Capa round, at least not on to any battle fields. There's enough of that with Beth." Then Ted reflects, "And I had enough of my younger brother, Georgie, pestering me. I will be well behaved." Ted turns to Capa with a eagerness, a hunger: "Look, one of the things I'd like to ask, if its not being rude, is about your name. I've heard people say Capa is a stage name." Capa raises his eyebrows. "Oh," Ted continues, "no critique of your integrity. It's just my "Ted Allan" is a pen name." There is an expectant pause. "It's a long story."

"Tell it," says Capa.

"I was a journalist in Montreal, my home, and the mayor, and the archbishop, even though they are very right wing, they let me know that Arcand, our own local Fuhrer, is being bankrolled out of Berlin. That called for some investigative journalism, I thought, but I couldn't use a Jewish name to join the fascists. I was Alan Herman. So some Ted Allan joined the fascists for as few weeks. I never got to see their secrets, but the name stuck."

"Finding my name wasn't so romantic. I was Andre Friedmann, and... and it was Gerda's idea."

Gerda explains, "People are going to have prejudgment, a prejudice of you. You have to give them a name, a name they can respect, if you want to successful, to do business with them. In Paris I was Robert's photographic assistant and his student. He wasn't making money. The Parisians did not trust a Mr. Friedmann. And Girta Pohorylle, who is she?"

"And Gerda Taro, who is she?" asks Ted.

"I am," says Gerda preening.

INTERIOR: TED'S ROOM AT THE BLOOD TRANSFUSION UNIT: NIGHT. Ted is typing at the Royal portable typewriter that Beth has given him. We watch over his shoulder, zoom in on what he is writing, and hear the young Ted's Voice Over (V.O.) the clickity clack. "Gerda says I have fallen in love with Capa. I could easily fall in love with her: "Capa's girl". The Spaniards call her *la pequeña rubia* , the little blonde. She's really more of a redhead. More copper than gold."

Ted pulls the cartage return lever, "dring", and starts typing a new paragraph. "I'm doing my first radio broadcast tomorrow! Interviewing Bethune. What shall I ask him?"

INTERIOR: A RADIO STUDIO IN THE TELEFONICA BUILDING, MADRID. NIGHT. Ted and Bethune with great big earphones in front to great big microphones. Ted asks, "Why are you here?"

"The fascists are monsters," says Bethune. "I was in Almeria when they bombed the refugee from Malaga, women and children who had escaped them. They left the port alone. That might be a legitimate target, but they left that untouched. Attacked the civilian population. They are monsters. They must be stopped."

Bethune continues, "What is the best I can do for the resistance, to smash fascism? I had the thought, "I could bring blood right to the frontline. It can be done. I can do that. Transfusions at the field hospitals. It will save lives. It will raise morale. It could change the game, the camel's back." We must all contribute what we can. We can stop fascism. We <u>will</u> stop the Nazis. But you have to put yourself on the line. "¡No pasarán!". They shall not pass. We can do this! And if you know what can be done, what must be done, you have to set an example."

FADE TO: a wide angle shot of the Grand Via in Madrid. Morning. People on their way to work. The camera pans and dollies along the avenue, passed

bombed out lots and damaged buildings. Crew of workmen clearing up the damage of the night. Much is still intact, though.

We approach the front of the Hotel Florida. There is a small terrace with tables. We recognize CAPA and GERDA at one table. We watch TED approach the hotel. Capa sees him and waves. Ted sees his new friends and his face lights up. He goes over to greet them.

"Would you like to join us today?" asks Capa. Ted reaches for, and pulls back a chair to sit. "Ah, yes," says Capa, "for breakfast, but I meant for the day. We've booked a driver to take us to the Jarama. The front has stabilized, but we should still be able to get some useful pictures."

"That would be swell," says Ted, and as he continues Voice Over we DISSOLVE TO: a car driving through the country-side outside Madrid. "I'd like to try and find the lads I came over with. They're with the Lincoln Battalion.[2] I think they're on the Jarama.

DISSOLVE TO: TED, CAPA, GERDA walking across a gently sloping hillside. Halfway down the hill we see a soldier walking carrying his rifle in his right hand. We hear the occasional retort of gunfire.

"I think he is with the POUM[3]," says Gerda pointing.

---

[2] The Mackenzie–Papineau Battalion or Mac-Paps were a battalion was formed in May 1937. Before that Canadians served in the Lincoln Battalion.

[3] The Workers' Party of Marxist Unification (Spanish: *Partido Obrero de Unificación Marxista*, POUM;

"Beth and I think that the Trotskyites are maybe more dangerous than the fascists," says Ted.

Gerda shakes her head. "Good people must stand together."

"Right, right," says Ted. "Solidarity, but..." He too shakes his head.

"Let's get closer," says Capa.

"There may be snipers," Ted cautions.

"If the photo isn't good enough, you weren't close enough," Capa scolds. "We'll be careful," he says, meaninglessly, angling down the gentle incline obliquely towards the soldier.

Gerda has a photographer's bag slung over a shoulder and a Rolliflex, a bulky, box-shaped "reflex" camera, hung round her neck. Capa has smaller, 35 mm, Leica, and film cartridges bulging in all his pockets. As they near the soldier, Capa stops and starts shooting. Almost at once the soldiers staggers, dropping his rifle. We hear the clack of a sniper's shot. The soldier collapses backward. Ted dives to the ground. Capa and Gerda run, crouched, to the soldier, kneel over him. They look at each other. Shake their heads. Then, still crouching, they move gingerly back up the hillside, beckoning Ted to follow. He rises, crouched, and runs.

"Holy shit!" says Ted.

DISSOLVE TO: interior of the taxi driving back towards Madrid. We find CAPA and GERDA in the backseat fussing with their photographer's bags and equipment. TED in the front, by the DRIVER, is ashen, is in shock. We hear the NARRATOR (V.O.): "We found the Lincoln Battalion, but none of my companions. They were all dead. Not a month had passed. All dead holding the line on the Jarama."

FADE TO: The Blood Transfusion Unit's ambulance pulling up sharply in front of a government office, perhaps even a screech of brakes. Bethune energetically emerges from the drivers door. He is dressed, immaculately, in a black battle

dress it seems. He has a briefcase in his hand. He strides towards the government office. Ted, Jean Watts, Henning Sise, emerge, like clowns, from the ambulance and follow sheepishly. Bethune salutes smartly the soldiers standing guard casually by the front entrance. The do not return his salute, but greet him, "*Hola.*"

DISSOLVE TO: Bethune bursts into Arturo Barea, the censor's, office followed by his reluctant entourage. Bethune is now brandishing a sheath of papers, waving them in Barea's direction, and ranting. "You see these! You see these! We found them in a locked desk drawer in the mansion on the Principe de Vergara. At the Unit! The Unit! They are German. German letters!"

Barea calmly holds out his hand. He starts to examine the documents. "I don't read German very well. We will have to get them translated. Let's see... the date is 1934." He shuffles through the letters on his desk. "'34, '33, '33. Perhaps there is no urgency here."

Bethune is indignant. "These are German. In a locked drawer. They could be anything. Espionage. Military, business secrets. They could be anything."

Barea repeats, but quietly, "They could be anything. We will look into it."

Bethune continues in his raised, agitated voice, "They could be important. This is no time for a siesta. Give them back to me! I'll take them to Alvarez del Vayo[4]" He abruptly wheels on his feet and stomps towards the door.

"Come," he orders his embarrassed followers.

Ted with his typewriter again, types, "Bethune is getting out of hand, a little. Drinking ever night, and raging far too often. Could Culebras and Gonzalez really be collaborators? It hardly seems possible. They're Party members. Am I being naive, or is Beth being paranoid. I don't know what to do. I may have to talk to the Party in Montreal about it. To Fred Rose, tabernac!"

Ted pulls the return lever, twice, "dring... dring" "On the other hand," he types, "Wow! Madrid is the centre of the universe. A large portion of the world's literary talent is here. Hemingway and Gellhorn. John Dos Passos. Everyone but Shakespeare. But I've said that before."

Another morning on the terrace of the Hotel Florida, Ted sits with his new friends, Capa and Gerda, their companion, Chim. (Another a made up name, this for David Seymour, a photographer, close friend of Gerda and Capa.) And this morning the novelist, John Dos Passos, sits with them. Ted is telling them about Beth storming out of Barea's office and how worried he is becoming about Beth's demeanour.

"Bethune was a close friend of yours in Montreal, yes?" says Capa.

---

[4] Alvarez del Vayo was the minister of Foreign Affairs

"Almost like a father. A colleague, a colleague, but almost like a father, a brother"

"How did you meet him?" Chim asks.

"It's a few years back," says Ted. "After I'd had my first short story published in a small magazine in Montreal. Bethune phoned me, out of the blue. Congratulated me, and invited me to his birthday party. When I arrived he led me to the bathroom! One of the bathroom walls was covered with all his diplomas. And another was covered in handprints. There was a pan of blue paint on a stool. He took my hand, thrust it in the bowl, in the paint. Then pressed it against the wall and said, "Sign it." "Ted Allan," I wrote, maybe the first time that I'd signed my new name, rather than typed it. "You are now numbered amongst my special friends," he told me, and we really have been quite close since then. Yeah. I like to think I may have influenced him in his decision to joint the Party."

"I take it you are a Party member," says Capa in his thick Hungarian accent.

"Hmm, well sort of," says Ted. "Alan Herman was a member of the Young Communists League, but I'm not sure that as a journalist I now want to actually be under Party discipline. Oh, I am in practice, but the principle is quite important. And here, in Spain, I report to the Brigade."

"So how long have you known Bethune?" asks Chim. Dos Passos just listens to the conversation.

"It'll be a little over three years," says Ted. "I'd just turned eighteen when I met Beth, when I changed my name."

"Robert," Ted continues, turning to Capa. "What do you make of Bethune?"

Capa thinks for a moment. "He rubs many people the wrong way."

"So true," says Ted. "Oh, and how long have you and Gerda been together?"

"We are not together," says Gerda. "We work together."

"We were together," says Capa.

"We are *copains*, companions" says Gerda.

"We are a team," says Capa.

At this point the conversation is interrupted by the arrival on the terrace of a small party in Brigade uniforms. Comrade Gallo and two armed "volunteers" escorting one small civilian figure. Gallo beckons to Ted. Ted excuses himself and rises to join them.

"You are looking for me?" Ted asks, a little incredulously.

"Oh, we are well informed," says Gallo lightly. "This gentleman says he is Martin Feldman of Montreal. He says he is in Madrid on "business". He says you will know him."

"Hi Alan," says Marty. He speaks with a Yiddish accent. "You remember me. Zelda's boy."

"Do you know this man?" asks Gallo.

"I've seen him round."

"What do you know about him?"

"He speaks Yiddish."

"And?"

"I don't know. I'm pretty sure he's Zelda's son. Zelda played poker with my mother."

"That's it? That's all?"

Ted holds his hand apart and shrugs an "I don't know." gesture.

"Gracia," says Gallo, and makes a gesture for his party to leave.

"What was that about," asks Capa as Ted returns.

Ted shrugs again. "Someone from Montreal who says he knows me." Capa raises his eye brows. Cocks his head. Ted continues, "And you'll excuse me a moment. I've got to visit the can."

DISSOLVE TO: Ted entering the men's room. Hemingway is there already standing peeing at the middle of the several urinals. Ted goes to the urinal furthest away. Hemingway notices him. Says, "Oh, hi there, kid.:"

"Hi there, Mr. Hemingway."

"You can call me "Papa". All my friends call me Papa."

"I know."

"Hey kid, Martha tells me you write short stories."

"Yeap."

"Could I read one?

"Sure," says Ted, now with some enthusiasm.

"Yeah. Bring me a couple of your short stories."

"Sure thing."

Hemingway has gone over to the wash basins, washing his hands, examining himself in the mirror.

There is a rumbling, crashing sound and a physical rumble and shaking of the building. It has been hit with an artillery shell. Not an infrequent event. "Well," says Hemingway, "one good thing about the shells hitting the hotel is it's getting rid of the Jews."

"What do you mean, "It's getting rid of the Jews"?"

"Well, I heard Herb Kline was leaving, and he mentioned three Jewish guys who had been in the hotel and they were leaving."

"Didn't you know I was Jewish?" says Ted.

"Oh Christ. I didn't remember you were Jewish."

"Yeah, I'm Jewish."

"Oh shit." Hemingway stands there a moment with his brow furrowed.   "Hey, you know what, kid? When you write your Spanish Civil War novel, I don't care how good or bad it is, I'll write a preface for it."

"Wow," say Ted. "That's great."

"It's a promise."

We watch Ted walking back to the Blood Transfusion Unit through the streets of Madrid, and hear the NARRATOR (V.O.) "It was a week or so later at lunch when Hemingway said, in front of everybody, "I read your stories, kid." "Yeah?" "I guess I don't have anything to worry about." I said, "Yeah, well I didn't think you'd have anything to worry about." "Yeah," he said. "You know what you should do with your stories?" "Yeah, what?" He said, "You should put then away for ten to twenty years, and then come back to them." I said, "Yeah, okay, thanks." And this was at the lunch table with everybody listening. I thought he was being pretty shit ass."

Ted hitches a ride on the running board of a passing car.

The NARRATOR (CONT'D V.O.) "Later, in New York, I brought Hemingway my first novel, THIS TIME A BETTER EARTH. I went back, a week later, with Martha Gellhorn to pick up the preface from Hemingway. "I wouldn't put my name on this rubbish," said "Papa". "Gerda was a whore!" "

"In the lobby of the hotel, when we were leaving, Martha said to me, "Ernest can be an asshole. And he can't even get it up. There! The secret life of Ernest Hemingway. Is that some consolation?"

" "I guess," I said."

In Madrid, in our movie, Ted jumps off the running board. Goes into the grounds of the Blood Transfusion Unit. There is commotion in the forecourt, the last stages of loading up the ambulances. Bethune waves to Ted. Ted gets into the ambulance with Beth and Sise. They drive off.

Meanwhile, the NARRATOR (CONT'D V.O.) "Then, decades later I got a call from a doctoral student at Dalhousie, researching "Canadian writing on Spanish Civil War". He wanted to discuss the possibility of re-issuing THIS TIME A BETTER EARTH[ii]. I mentioned that I'd come round to calling the work NEXT TIME A BETTER BOOK.

""Oh, I found it a page turner," he said. "You know that both your book, published in 1939, and Hemingway's Spanish Civil War book, published in 1940, start with the hero riding in the back of a truck coming into Spain over the Pyrenees"."

EXTERIOR: A FIELD HOSPITAL. DAY. The Blood Transfusion Unit ambulance arrives. Bethune, Ted, Sise, get out. Bethune starts to triage. Sise and Ted set up the transfusion equipment.

The NARRATOR (CONT'D V.O.) "On the phone, I told the guy, the Dalhousie student, professor, that Hemingway had refused to write a promised preface for the novel.

" "That's interesting," he said. "There were two copies of *This Time a Better Earth* in Hemingway's library when he died." "

We watch Bethune working with the wounded and listen to the NARRATOR (CONT'D V.O.) "Bethune was so caring with his patients. What a saint that sinner was. Oh! Oh, I've got tell the CODA to the Marty Feldman story, the kid Gallo brought to me. I ran into him many years later on the streets of New York. He recognized me. "You," he said. "Why didn't you protect me?" "I hardly know you," I said. "They might have killed me." "They obviously didn't." "They could have killed me." "I trusted Gallo," I said. "We are Jewish," he said, and spat at my feet. And walked off."

FADE TO: Bethune at the Unit, drinking, night. The NARRATOR (CONT'D V.O.) "When Beth wasn't working, he was drinking, fighting with the Spanish staff."

Beth gets up, walks out of the building, gets into one of the ambulances. The NARRATOR (CONT'D V.O.) "Sometimes, when things were quiet on the battle fields, he'd just take off in the middle of the night in one of the Unit's ambulances. We might not see him for days. "Something has to be done," I told the Party in Montreal."

INTERIOR; THE BAR, HOTEL FLORIDA: NIGHT. The bar is crowded. The camera dollies (and pans) passed Hemingway and Gellhorn. Hemingway is saying, "That Ted Allan's a party hack. And his short stories aren't worth a dime." Gellhorn says, "Oh, I think he shows some promise," and Papa says, "So I hear."

The camera pans and in the middle ground we see Ted, Capa and Gerda sitting together. We zoom in on their table. Capa is holding a copy of *Paris Match*.[iii] On the front cover is the picture he took of the POUM soldier falling. Capa and Gerda are obviously pleased.

Ted is again the enthusiast. "That is amazing! That is just wonderful," he says.

"Yes," says Capa. "We came here to bring Spain to the attention of the well intentioned masses."

"People," says Gerda interrupting and correcting Capa.

Capa nods. "Now we can go to China."

"You're going to China?" says Ted with surprise.

"The Japanese are poised to invade from Manchuria. Only Mao Tse Tung's Communist China will stand in their way. Chiang Kai-shek will run and hide."

"Mao is very interesting," says Gerda. "He has built a people's state away from the government that has the power, will have the power to topple the government. The Japanese will expand, will invade, and only Mao will stand against them."

"Are you going to China?" Ted asks Gerda.

"I think so. It's a story that needs to be told. You should come too."

"I have to deal with Bethune," says Ted. "And I am under the orders of the Brigade. I report to the Brigade."

"Ask the Brigade if you can report to them on Mao," Gerda quips.

"And what is happening with Bethune?" asks Capa.

"Oh!" Ted expostulate vehemently. "Oi!" he says more playfully. "More drunken tantrums, a broken window, thrown…"

"A broken window?" asks Gerda.

"He slammed the door so hard the window in the door shattered. There was a chair he threw across the room. He flings ashtrays. Another episode absconding in the night with one of the ambulances last week. Gone for three days. I find myself allied now with people Bethune calls "the misfits and the shits". And I'm afraid now I agree that he has to leave the Unit. I've written a report, copies to the Brigade and to the Party in Canada, suggesting Bethune be sent home. In Spain he has become a liability. In Canada he could be of service, speaking, and raising money for the Spanish Aid Committee."

"You should send him to China," says Gerda.

"Hmph," says Ted. "I'll mention it. to him. He says that he is planning to go to Valencia next week to buy medical supplies, he says. Any excuse to get away, because we all know there are no medical supplies in Valencia. That will work out just fine, though, because the Canadian Party is sending over some bigwigs, worthies to investigate. They can come to the Unit while Beth's away; meet with the Unit's personnel and hear it all for themselves."

"You should send Beth to China," Gerda reiterates.

"Well," says Capa. "I want to raise a toast to our trip to China." He lifts his glass.

"To the end of fascism in Europe and Asia," says Ted raising his.

"So Teddy," says Capa. "I'm off to Paris next week to start making arrangement for our trip. Gerda will join me at the end of the month. That's the plan. Meanwhile I leave her in your care. Look after her for me."

Gerda has a little look of consternation on her face.

Ted just smiles. "Of course."

FADE TO: Ted typing on Bethune "Royal" portable. "The party is sending over
A.A. MacLeod and William Kashtan to make some decisions about Beth. I'm glad it's out of my hands..."

DISSOLVE TO: An older Ted, the NARRATOR, at his electric typewriter in his apartment overlooking the Thames at Putney, London. We hear the NARRATOR (V.O.) tell us, "Most of the story, up until now, till I brought up China, was actual, factual, historical. Oh, I've invented, reinvented some of the dialogue, but it's been as near the truth as I could manage as the story teller I am. The China theme, though, is a fiction. A self-aggrandizing fiction, even. Why muddle the story? Why pretend Gerda and I sent Bethune to China? Well, I figure, people aren't going to believe the truth anyway. There are some who won't believe me whatever I say. So I might as well give them some meat with the potatoes. Hey, and... it's my movie."

FADE TO: INTERIOR: OFFICE AT THE BLOOD TRANSFUSION UNIT: DAY.
The office is a large room – not a ballroom, but not far off - in the mansion on the Principe de Vergara. Now it's furnished with office equipment. Three of the desks sport the Unit's three typewriter. There is an alcove, curtained off from the main room, where the refrigerators are housed.

Kashtan and MacLeod, the worthies from Montreal, are at the head of the room with Ted. The rest of the Unit's staff, that is the two Spanish doctors, several nurses, several orderlies, a janitor, a driver, Sise and another Canadian volunteer, and Jean Watts, the journalist, who has been staying at the Unit: altogether they pretty much fill the room.

We watch a MONTAGE of short clips of the individuals giving testimony, DISSOLVING one into the next (linked to what we are hearing) as we listen to the NARRATOR tell us: "So, a few days later, with Bethune gone off to Valencia in one or the ambulances "for supplies", the staff of the Unit met with Kashtan and MacLeod to discuss the status of the Unit and what should be done about Bethune. Everyone spoke. HENNING SISE translated, both the Spanish to English and English into Spanish."

NARRATOR (CONT'D V.O.): "Jean Watts confessed she wasn't a member of the team, only a guest in the house, but maintained that as a reporter she had some objectivity, and then she spoke with fervent emotion of how she'd come to "hate" Bethune, how he was "a complete insensitive megalomaniac". We didn't use the word sexist in those days, but that's what she implied. Beth wasn't sexist *per se*; but he was in your face, and he called your bullshit. He called Jim, (we called Jean Jim) he called her on her bullshit. Actually I think what got her goat was that he didn't fancy her.

"Then Dr. Culebras ranted, sawing the air with a pumping elbow like Adolph Hitler himself, barely acknowledging Sise's attempts to translate."

"Culebras's sister, the nursing nun, gave a melodramatic soliloquy crossing herself and appealing to the heavens."

"Only Henning spoke positively of the great work that Bethune had accomplished and the great pressures he was under."

"On and on the meeting went, slowed by the translation: load upon load of loud complaint. "A liability." "Out of control." Oh, and et cetera."

"Finally it was my turn to speak; to sum up. "We all know he can be a son of a bitch..." I began, and as I started, Bethune, who had not gone to Valencia, who had hidden in the alcove, pushed the curtain aside and emerged with an "et tu, Brute?" stare that stabbed me. He pierced me with his glare long moments..."

BETHUNE, shakes his head, sadly, despondently. Turns his back on Ted. Walks through the office. The staff watch, motionless. Beth looks neither left nor right. He walks straight from the office, down the hall, retiring to his room.

Ted, then Kashtan and MacLeod, follow. Ted follows Bethune into his room, but turns and closes the door on the two worthies following.

CUT TO: TED and BETHUNE face each other.

"You think nothing of the faith I've vested in you?" says Bethune adamantly. "You care nothing for that trust?"

"Beth. I'm totally.... You've been like a father to me."

"Behind my back!"

"You can't stay here, Beth. There's too much friction, too much luggage. And there's no other way. There's no way through. You go home."

"You're ordering me!"

"I can't, and wouldn't, "order" you, Beth. But the Party wants you to go home."

"Culebras is a saboteur and a spy!"

"We can't prove that."

"Move him out of the unit. Don't shoot the bastard! Side-step him."

"It can't be done."

"Ask Gallo."

"Gallo's the Brigade. He's not the government. And Culebras is in the Party. He's out-flanked you. And you've made enemies, Beth."

"Gallo?"

"No. No. He thinks the world of you. No, Barea. Barea thinks you are an ass. And others. And others. Beth. Go home. Raise money for the refugees."

There's a pause, Bethune glaring. Then Ted continues, "Gerda Taro says you should go to China. "Go see Mao," she says. "Put those two together and they'll move the world." That's what she said."[iv]

Ted continues, quietly, "Beth. Go home."

And Beth mutters, musingly. "Son of a bitch," he says. "Son of a bitch!"

A LONG FADE OUT. Over a darkening screen we hear NORMAN (V.O.) say, "If I were to introduce myself in this story, into this movie, me the author, scriptwriter, it would be sitting with Ted in his flat in Putney, above the river. Me in my thirty, he's turning sixty, him telling me…"

FADE IN: An elderly Ted, the NARRATOR, sits by the picture window overlooking the Thames. He tells us, "Bethune was the most exciting person I ever met. And he was like a father to me.

It changed me, knowing him. Brought me into a wider world. A validation, that's the word. Ah, but things were cold between us when I saw him next back in Canada. Oh, he dressed my wound a couple of times, but he didn't forgive me.

DISSOLVE TO: TED walking with GERDA through a Spanish village, Gerda photographing the villagers, the children.

      NARRATOR (CONT'D V.O.): "Decades later I received a visit from an attaché with the Spanish embassy. He told me they had opened Franco's "intelligence" archives; were going through them, and they'd discovered that doctors Culebras and Gonzalez were indeed fascist spies and saboteurs. Beth was right about that. Do I feel guilty? Yes."

      NARRATOR (CONT'D V.O.): "Ah, but back in the movie, with Capa gone to Paris, and Bethune back to Canada, I started spending almost all my time with Gerda."

      On the screen we've watched the villagers offering the Ted and Gerda refreshments; wine and bread and olives. Now they sit beneath an olive tree. Nod to villagers, but conversation falters after a toast of "¡No pasarán!"; "¡No pasarán!"

      Gerda and Ted start to talk among themselves. Ted, "This is beautiful. Who would think there was a war?"

      Gerda, "What will you do after the war."

      "I'll follow you. I'll look after you, if you let me. And I'll write plays."

      "You'll write for the theatre?"

      "I hope so. I study Chekov, Ibsen."

      "Shakespeare?"

"I study the Bard, but no one can write like Shakespeare. But in my little way I think I've figured some of it out."

"Some of what?"

"The laws of drama."

"The laws of drama?"

"Yes. I've found, or I know, the first three laws of drama."

"Yes?"

"The first law of drama is that there has to be conflict. Without conflict there's no story, no drama."

"Ah," says Gerda. "That explains it. That may explain why there is the evil in the world." She waves her hand at the sky. "God was in His renaissance heaven sitting on His throne, surrounded by His angels singing hallaluja and hosanna for eternity, and God said "Enough! Let there be dark, and light." Yes, that's it. The source of sin: a random universe. And the second law?"

"The second law: there has to be character development."

Gerda makes a closed fist salute, "Yes, comrade! Yes!"

"Don't tease me," says Ted.

"No, no, no. Indeed the wise say we are here to grow, to learn. And the third law?"

"You've got to care. The audience has got to identify with the story."

Gerda, "And in the story God writes, we identify because we are the hero in our own little story."

Ted shrugs. "Those are my three laws."

"The fourth and five laws," says Gerda, "of drama, of the theatre, stage plays, I think, is that the climax must be totally predictable and at the same time a complete surprise."

Gerda sits a moment thinking, and then adds, "Law number six: the author should not be on the stage. That's why the devine hides."

"Hides where?" Ted asks.

"A burning bush in the mind," say Gerda.

"Ah," says Ted. "And the seventh law is love."

Gerda claps. Gerda smiles.

Ted smiles back, and then, remembering, adds, "Oh, and I told Beth what you said, how he and Mao could move the world."

"Well it's true," says Gerda.

DISSOLVE TO: GERDA'S HOTEL ROOM, DAY. GERDA is sitting up on the bed reading Ted's short stories. Ted sits, rather anxiously, fidgety, in a chair.

NARRATOR (V.O.): "For weeks Gerda and I spent mornings, afternoons and evenings together chasing stories of interest - battlefields, orphanages, women lining up for bread. Driving to or from the front we would sing. She taught me many revolutionary songs; "die Moorsoldatan", "Freihejt!", "Los cuatro generales" ("heneralis", we sang with gusto).

"Gerda was always joyful, always laughing. We'd become constant companions. And finally, one afternoon, we ended up in her hotel room. I had brought Gerda my short stories to read."

"With Martha Gellhorn I had pushed my stories on her right away. With Gerda, where I really cared, I was more restrained. There in her room I sat on a chair trying to look unconcerned. She read slowly. Finally she looked up. "You're good," she said. I felt dizzy."

Gerda walks to the bathroom. The camera follows. She slips off her shirt and skirt, undressing to her underwear. She returns to the room brushing her teeth, seemingly unaware of her state of undress. She wanders back to the bathroom to rinse her mouth, and ambles back into the room again.

We hear the NARRATOR echo over the action, " "You're very good," she repeated, staring at me." At the same time we hear Gerda too, on screen, say "You're very good.".

NARRATOR (CONT'D V.O.): "I tried not to look at her bra or panties,"

Gerda goes and lies down on the bed. Ted sits in his chair. Gerda asks, "Do you feel like taking a nap before we go to dinner?". She pats the bed. "Come."

Ted moves to the bed, removes his shoes, and lies beside her, making sure their bodies don't touch. He lies there stiffly watching the ceiling.

Gerda turns on her side and touches Ted's right eye-lid with her finger tip. "A man shouldn't have such eyes," she says.

"I'm not queer," says Ted.

"No no no, just beautiful eyes," says Gerda. She touches Ted's cheek, then lies back on her back and burst out, "I'm not going to fall in love again! It's too painful." She sounded irritated.

"What do you mean?"

"I loved someone. A boy in Prague. Tortured and murdered by the Gestapo. It's too painful." She takes a deep breath.

"You don't love Capa?" Ted asks, puzzled.

"We've been through this. I do love Capa, but not the way I loved Georg. I don't want to love anybody like I loved Georg. Capa is my friend, my *copain*."

She looks at the ceiling. Ted turns his head to study her. Their bodies are not quite touching, but Ted moves away quickly when he feels that their hips might be touching. Then he lies still again. Moments pass.

Gerda places her hand on Ted's stomach. She studies him, then moves her hand to his thigh, near his groin. "Do you like being touched here?" she asks.

Ted nods quickly, then nods again. He holds his breath.

She takes Ted's hand and placed it in her groin. "I like to be touched there too."

Ted caresses her gently, carefully, hardly moving. Then he withdraws his hand and stares at the ceiling again.

Gerda turns on her side and studied Ted. "You're incredible," she says. She sits up. "I'd better dress." She looks at Ted, touches his cheek, bends down and kisses his forehead. She smiles an enigmatic a smile..

Ted starts to speak, "I… I," then pauses. "I like women," he begins. "I've been with women, and girls. And I love you. But Capa is my best friend."

"I thought "best friend" implied little, a little permanence."

"Hey, we're young, and there's a war on. We have to make quick decisions. But…" He catches himself, stops and starts again, "I mean <u>and</u> I love you, so we've got to get it right.""

"We're young, and there is war that needs fighting. Yes, so we've got to get it right." Gerda looks sad. She sighs. She gets out of bed and starts dressing.

Ted lies on the bed, seemingly stunned.

Gerda finishes dressing.

Ted sits up, puts on his shoes. Then sits there a moment, a dazed look on his face before asking, "Are you going to marry Capa?"

Gerda gives an exasperated sigh. Shakes her head. "I told you, five times now, he's my *copain*, not my lover. He still wants us to marry, but I don't want to."

Ted sits still on the edge of the bed. Gerda moves close. Stands in front of him.

CLOSE UP: Ted on the edge of tears, smiling to hide it.

Gerda touches Ted's head. Ted says, "He acts like you are lovers. He put you in my charge. He asked me to take care of you."

Gerda sighs. "Yes. He was clever. He saw how I looked at you."

"Uh, um," Ted stutters again

"What?"

"I … I don't know how to…"

"Ask"

"Hemingway said you were "a loose woman"."

"Hemingway has a bruise on his shin and his ego. I think I may have broken some of his toes."v

Ted stands, close now to Gerda, silent a moment, and then blurts out, "My mother will love you."

Without a pause, Gerda says, "I don't want to live in Montreal."

"We could live in New York."

"I could live in New York," she echoes.

The NARRATOR (V.O.): "We said no more, but went to dinner. I think I was in shock."

AERIAL SHOT: A TAXI DRIVING THROUGH THE COUNTRYSIDE. DAY.

CUT TO: an establishing interior shot of a Spanish driver in front and TED and GERDA in the back of the taxi. They are holding hands, calmly. Gerda asks the taxi driver, *"Conoces Los Cuatros Generales?"*

"Si."

"Cantarias con nosotros?"

"Okey-Dookey," says the drive and he starts to bellow, *"Los cuatro generales."* Gerda and Ted happily sing along… *"Los cuatro generales, Los cuatro generales, Mamita mia, Que se han alzado, Se han alzado…"*

(Subtitles: The four insurgent generals… Mamita mia, They tried to betray us…)

As the singing starts, and it will go on for many verses, we hear the NARRATOR (V.O.) say, "The next day, the 25th of July, 1937, the day before Gerda was to return to Paris, to meet up with Capa… was she going to China with Capa, or going to tell him she was staying with me? We didn't discuss it. We just smiled. We just smiled. But she wanted to get pictures of the battle."

Below the narration Gerda, Ted, and the driver continue to sing: *"Madrid, que bien resistes, Madrid, que bien resistes, Madrid, que bien resistes, Mamita mia, Los bombardeos, Los bombardeos."*

NARRATOR (CONT'D. V.O.) "For nearly three weeks there had been fierce fighting to the west of Madrid. The Republicans, the Loyalists, had launched a major offensive to relieve Madrid of its near encirclement. We had taken several villages and the town of Brunete. Fierce fighting. For weeks. Terrible casualties. But yesterday the Nationalists, the fascists, had retaken the town, been driven out again, retaken it, perhaps. The battle in flux. The last place I wanted to be, but Gerda wanted her pictures."

DISSOLVE TO: the taxi has stopped in the countryside. Gerda and Ted are bidding farewell to the driver. The taxi drives off, and as the splutter of its engine noise recedes, we hear the wind. A forlorn sound for this middle distance shot of Ted and Gerda in a desolate landscape. Far in the distance we see a small town or village. And now we hear occasional sounds of war.

Gerda has the Leica that Capa has given her to replace her cumbersome Rolliflex… she has the Leica slung around her neck. Ted is carrying her movie camera and her photographer's bag.

"Where are the lines?" Ted asks.

"Just over this hill, I think."

"That's close."

"That's good."

"Let's not go too close."

"How do you want me to take pictures? Long distance?"

"That's an idea," says Ted.

"You know what Capa says," *la pequeña rubia* teases. "Are you frightened?" she asks.

"Oh yes. Aren't you?"

Gerda laughs, "Oh yes," and starts, straight off, walking up the rise through the wheat field. As they top the rise we look down, at some distance, on a small cemetery. We can see soldiers, small in the distance like tin soldiers, dug in there. "Those are ours," says Gerda, pointing.

Now we notice a group of officers walking rapidly in the general direction of Ted and Gerda, and we see that they are close by a dug-out. "It's your friend, General Walter," says Ted. "We interviewed him last week."

The General sees them, diverts his path to approach them. He is not pleased. "Of all days to come," he groans. He speaks with a Polish accent.[vi] "You must go away immediately. Go back. Go right back!" He stepped forward right into Ted's face. "Get her away from here."

"What!" Gerda complains. "I am going to Paris tomorrow. This is my last chance. I must stay!"

"No!" the General barks. "Take her away from here. Go immediately. I can't be responsible for you. In five minutes there will be hell!" Then General Walter dismisses them from his attention, and marches off, with his adjutants, to the dug-out, his headquarters.

"Let's go. Come," says Ted.

"You can go. I'm staying."

"But the General said... Ordered!"

Gerda gives Ted's comment a dismissive raised eyes nod. "To hell with General Karol." Gerda is adamant.

"Okay," Ted concedes. "Okay. You're crazy. Let's find some cover. There are some more dugouts on the hillside there, I think."

They walk through the field. Gerda points. They hustle, crouched, to a small dug out hollow, the earth mounded low on the down side of the hill, facing the enemy lines. The NARRATOR tells us, "We snuggled into a hole barely big enough to hide our two asses. We waited. Looked around. Other soldiers were precariously dug in around us."

Then we heard the drone of planes, and see a flight, approaching from the distance, like geese, twelve bombers in formation. We can see the tiny pursuit planes, fighters, flying like flies around the bombers. The drone becomes louder, becomes a roar. They appear to move so slowly, and then too soon they are dropping their bombs, which fall so quickly. Then it is thunder, black clouds billowing, about a hundred yards in front of Ted and Gerda, erupting and thundering again and again.

Gerda is busy taking pictures. Ted is fussing around, trying top find something with which to dig the hole deeper. He ends up using his hands. The bombs roar, thunder, and the earth showers round them..

"Put your head down!" Gerda yells.

"Where'll I put it? I can't pull it into my chest."

"Put it down! Put it down!"

The NARRATOR (V.O) tells us, "I don't think I can find words to fit the confusion and the fear, dirt, dust, the acrid smoke. It went on and on." And it goes on and on. Then, then there's a lull. The air clears. The stuttering drone of the planes becomes dimmer, thinner.

"Are you all right?" Ted asks.

"Who me? Sure. You?"

"Swell," says Ted.

Heads begin to appear in the foxholes, soldiers, some grinning, some grim. But then the planes return. The drone grow to a roar. Bombs a little more distant, though, this time..

SLOW DISSOLVE: TED and GERDA huddled in their hole. Again a lull in the air, though artillery shell continue to fall intermittently: intermittently, but also uninterruptedly.

Ted rolls onto his back. Gazes at the sky. Gerda to shifts to her back, watching the sky overhead.

NARRATOR (V.O): "It was three o'clock when the bombardment started. An eternity later it was suddenly quiet."

On screen Gerda asks, "What time is it?"

"Four. A bit after."

Gerda has managed to get her feet underneath Ted. "When the planes come again you had better watch your head," she says. "Shrapnel, you know."

"I know. But you're taking pictures and your head is above the ground."

"Yes, but I must take pictures and you don't have to."

"I'm scared out of my wits."

"Teddie, hon. I can't give you my attention right now. I'm working."

"Can I talk to you about drama?"

"What… (pause) … about drama."

"I think the story has to have a moral… has to be a reason for telling it. But I don't know what the moral of *Hamlet* is."

Gerda says, "I know the moral of *Lear*."

"Yes?"

"If you are a stupid vain fool, you may rue it," says Gerda, and continues, "*Othello*: listen to false counsel and doubt love is the road to perdition. You say "perdition"?"

"Yes, and *Hamlet*."

"Don't get caught up in other people's business," advises Gerda. "And if you do get tangled up in their problems, run."

"So Hamlet is doomed unless he runs?" says Ted.

"No, I've got that wrong," says Gerda. "How can he run from the murder of his father? Hamlet is doomed because he lets religious superstition stay his hand."

"And hatred, and vengeance," says Ted. "He didn't want Claudius to end up in heaven if he killed him while he was praying."

"And hatred and vengeance. You're sharp," says Gerda.

"Wow," says Ted. "Let's tempt fate. The *Tempest*?"

"Conjure magic," says Gerda. "Let love rule... even the fool."

""I don't see it," says Ted.

Gerda does not reply, returns her attention to the job at hand, attending to and recording the moment. She props herself up on her elbows, looking around and occasionally snapping a photograph.

"Gerda," says Ted, trying to catch her attention. She doesn't look round. She's peering over the small earthen mound. "Gerda. Gerda," Ted pesters like a child. She looks at him, and looks heavenward. "I figured the moral of Oedipus Rex," he says, and receives an indulgent half smile. "If you kill a stranger at the crossroads," he continues, "you might just unhinge, or shake the whole moral fabric of the universe."

Gerda rewards this with a smile. "Cute," she says.

"You know I came here in part to be with Bethune."

She takes her attention back to the landscape and her camera.

"I could come to Paris with you." No response. "What we have to do is wake up the masses," says Ted.

"Masses, masses," says Gerda. "We need to think about the whole people. Everybody."

"The world is a madness," says Ted. "The tyranny is as old as civilization."

"So we must wake up the people, all the people."

"Like Jesus?"

"We'd better do better then that," Gerda says

"Where would you start?" Ted asks

"Paris. New York. What's in New York?

"I don't know," says Ted,

"It's a big mouth," says Gerda.

"It's The Big Apple," says Ted"

It's a big mouth," says Gerda. "I don't know how I can photograph that."

They lie there a while.

This is the European art film bit. We watch ants moving through the dirt. Wind moving through the wheat. Birds winging, long shot across the whole sky, then the bird explodes. Then we hear the shot. And once more a brief silence.

And at this point now again we heard the drone of aircraft growing, though this time with a different timbre. A flight of bi-planes flying low swings towards the camera. Gerda clicks her Leica as the first plane turns on its side and bellies in towards them. We hear the rat-tat-tat of machine gun fire. One by one the bi-planes strafe the Republican lines, earth spurting not that far, and sometimes quite close, to the camera. Nine planes in all and with almost no interruption the first comes back, and then the rest, to make a second pass.

Barely have the fighter planes gone when the bombers return, bomb the lines again. And still the artillery shells fall round us. "It must end sometime," says Ted. Gerda doesn't answer, takes pictures of the smoke and the black earth heaving with each bomb. She snaps the dust and smoke, picture after picture. Ted crouches there.

Then, "Scheise!" says Gerda suddenly with some urgency. "They must have seen my lens flash in the sun. Put your head down!" The planes meanwhile have swung right at us, right at the camera. The NARRATOR (V.O.) tells us, ""Bloody German Condor Legion vultures: "volunteer" pilots from Germany, whole squadrons of them, Mein Gott. And it had become personal. We were their specific target. The lead plane came gently towards us. There was a surge to the sound of its engine," which we hear and watch. NARRATOR (CONT'D V.O.) "and a stuttering flashing through the propellers, and the earth in front of our foxhole jumped in spurts."

Gerda, unshaken, takes pictures of the planes as they come down on and over us. "Yesus, the roll is finished." She rolls on to her back, and starts to change films. The planes roared over just a few yards above them. Gerda's movie camera, in its leather case, lies just beside the foxhole. Ted grabs for the movie camera and holds it above her head to protect her from the machine gun bullets. "Don't be silly," she hissed. "I may lose my film. Teddie, don't put the camera over my head."

"Why not?"

"If we die here, it will be while trying to get these pictures, yes?" Gerda has to yell to be heard.

"Yes."

"Then they are very valuable."

"Yes."

"Look after them."

"Capa told me to look after <u>you</u>."

"Yes," yells Gerda.

"Yes," says Ted. "General Walter said to get you out of here."

"Yes," says Gerda. "Who do you love?"

"I love you."

"Then continue to look out for me, and look after the film."

"Yes, yes," mouths Ted. "The photographer's bag. The film canisters. Yes"

Through this a showering of dirt, from the strafing, continues to on them, splattering them. Gerda allows Ted to continue holding the camera over her head. Now Ted, with his other hand, grabs a clod of earth and holds it just above his head. We hear a suppressed giggle. Gerda's body is shaking, with laughter. "If you could only see yourself," she splutters. But the nightmare continues: bombs, machine-guns, shells. Cacophony.

DISSOLVE TO A WIDER SHOT: we see GERDA and TED in their foxhole, and the hillside and the Republican lines in front of them. We watch and listen while the NARRATOR (V.O.) tells us, "Suddenly on the slope in front of us we saw men running back towards us. They were retreating all up and down the line. If that were possible, it seemed the bombardment intensified. We saw men blown into the air, just like in the movies, but real, just there in front of us. You could touch it. Gerda put another roll into her Leica and rolled over to shoot the onrushing retreat. I felt desperate. I didn't know what was more maddening then, the planes or the clicking of her camera."

NARRATOR (CONT'D V.O.): "One section of the lines was orderly and the retreat went comparatively smoothly. But a retreat is a retreat, and even though it was not a rout, there was confusion. Men get panicky and run anywhere as long as they can run. In front of us a few took position with there guns pointed back towards the enemy, and seemed to dare anyone to pass them. This stopped the panic. The lines reformed."

On camera Ted pleads to Gerda, "Come, for God's sakes. Let's go!"

"Not now while the planes are still strafing. It would be silly to go now.. And anyways, I have one roll left."

NARRATOR (CONT'D V.O.): "Then again it was quiet. Very quiet. Here and there a figure moved. A cool breeze came down from the mountains. The wheat swayed gently Above the hills clouds puffed and drifted by. The countryside looked serene."

On camera Gerda says abruptly, rising, "Come, lets go."

"What?"

"Yes, I'm tired."

We watch, and listen as the NARRATOR tells us, "We got out of our rut, our foxhole. We walked back through a meadow away from the front, towards the village of Villanueva de la Cañada. The lines had reformed between the two villages, Brunete and Villanueva. We joined and followed the road. Beside the road lay the dead and wounded. Some groaned and begged for water. Some lay silent. Gerda had no more film."

NARRATOR (CONT'D V.O.): "The planes came again. We flung ourselves underneath an overturned truck. But the planes passed over. They weren't looking for us."

EXTERIOR: SPANISH ROADSIDE; DAY. Gerda and Ted walk along the road towards camera. We see a car approaching. Gerda flags it down. It comes to a stop. CLOSE SHOT: of Gerda and Ted approaching the drivers window, speak with the driver. We see the car is full with wounded Republican soldiers.

NARRATOR (V.O.): "A large black touring car came down the road. We stopped it and Gerda asked for a lift as far as El Escorial.

On screen the driver say, "*Seguro, si puede montar en el estribo, subase.*" (Subtitles: Sure. If you can ride on the running board, get on.)

Gerda asks, "*¿Podemos poner en el suelo las cámaras?*" (Subtitles: Can we put the cameras on the floor inside?)

NARRATOR (CONT'D V.O.): "The driver took the cameras and the photographer's bag through the window and stowed them on the floor somewhere. And Gerda said "Salud." to the wounded men inside – some grunted back - and we jumped on to the running board."

Gerda climbs on to the running board in front of Ted.

NARRATOR (CONT'D V.O.): "I suggested Gerda go to the other side. She demurred. "Why? It is big enough. We can both stay here." And off we went down the road."

NARRATOR (CONT'D V.O.): "Some planes came flying over again. They dived. Tat-tat-tat-tat."

And on screen we hear machine gun fire.

"Silly getting killed now after going through what we did," Ted yells.

"Bah, they can't hit a thing," Gerda yells back.

We watch the car roar and bounce along the way a while with just ambient noises, loud though they are. After a while Ted shouts, "Gerda, Gerda," to get her attention. She looks back. "I figured out the moral of Oedipus Rex," yells Ted.

"Yes, you told me."

"Oh," says Ted. Pauses a few beats then, "What do you think is the moral of <u>my</u> story?" he shouts.

"You did the right thing, at peril of your life, in coming here" says Gerda shouting just loud enough to be heard, "and you are being rewarded. The road to heaven is paved with good intentions," she adds.

"The saying is "the road to hell"."

"I know, but that's only in special cases. For you it is heaven."

"You're going to Paris tomorrow."

"I'm going to Paris <u>tomorrow</u>." She enunciates "tomorrow" carefully. Then adds, "I have to talk to Andre."

"Andre?"

"Capa."

A short silence ensues. The Gerda takes a deep breath and shouts above the wind, "Boy, that was a day. I feel swell. The lines reformed. I got wonderful pictures. And you? You have a good story, yes?"

"Swell."

"Tonight we'll have a farewell party in Madrid. I've bought some champagne. And we'll see each other in Paris? In any event, I am going to China, I think. With Capa, my *copain*, soon."

"I'd like to go to China too!" Ted shouts, "with you!"

"We'll see," says Gerda.

There is some confusion ahead on the road. A tank is approaching. It has just been strafed by a Nationalist plane and is driving erratically, weaving across the road. The staff car swings to the left to avoid it. "Hold on," Gerda laughs.

But the car begins to roll! The car rolls on to the drivers side, coming to a stop quite quickly in the sandy loam beside the road. We see Ted's body tumbling behind.

A CLOSE UP of Ted sitting behind the car, the car on its side. The wheels on the passenger's side, now up in the air, are still spinning.

NARRATOR (V.O.): "The car went out of control; began to roll. Then I was on the side of road. Then I knew that both my legs were off. Then I knew they weren't. I saw blood on my right leg. And the pants torn on my left. There was no pain.

"Gerda!" Ted screams. He tries to rise. He can't.

Two soldiers run towards him from the tank, which has now stopped in the middle distance.

"*¿Donde esta la mujer? La mujer! La mujer!*" shouts Ted. (Subtitles: Where is the woman? The woman!)

There are many gathered round the car now. Some are trying to lift the car, turn it back upright. The driver has managed to throw open the passenger's side door, is trying to lift himself out of car. Some of the soldiers round the car are shouting and gesticulating, telling him to wait. "¡ Espera! ¡ Espera! La mujer! ¡ Espera!" (Subtitles: Wait! The Woman. Wait!")

Ted, supported on each side by a soldier, hobbles towards the wreck.

NARRATOR (V.O.): "Then I saw her. I saw her face. Just her face. The rest of her body was hidden by the overturned car. She was screaming. Her eyes looked at me and asked me to help her. But I could not move. There was no pain, but I could not move on my own."

NARRATOR (CONT'D V.O.): "The tank was quiet now. It had swung around and now it was quiet. The young Spanish driver looked at us. He was frightened. Some soldiers, round the car, were trying to free Gerda. And then the planes came again. And the men beside me took me and dropped down to huddle in a ditch."

On camera Ted, crawling from the ditch, is screaming, "Gerda! Where are you? Gerda!" Ted is dragging his right leg. the thigh bone, the femur, is fractured[vii].

The planes go by.

"¿Donde esta la mujer?" Ted asks franticly. He is grimacing with pain, trying to stand (on one leg).

"La llevaron en una ambulancia," someone tells him. (Subtitles: She's been put into an ambulance.)

"What? What?"

" La llevaron en una ambulancia. Ambulancia. Ambulancia."

"Are you sure? Es verdad?"

"Si si."

"And her camera? Where is her camera?"

"*No se.*"

"In the car. *En el automóvil.*"

But the car has started to burn.

NARRATOR (V.O.): "Someone brought me a brown cloth belt. It was crumpled and the wooden buckle was crushed, smashed. "*Es la suya,*" (It is hers),said the someone. "*¿Dónde está el automóvil?*" (Where is the car?) I asked. "*Se esta quemando,*" (It is burning) they said. Then I was burning too. I'd begun to feel the pain. "*Agua. Water, I need water.*" But no one had water. They put me on a stretcher and placed me in an ambulance. There was no water. The pain became heavier. I held the brown belt in my hands. The buckle was broken! And soon, sometime I passed out."

EXTERIOR: AERIAL VIEW OF A CAR DRIVING THROUGH THE PYRENEES. DAY.

NARRATOR (V.O.): "I was in hospital for about a month. I'm hazy about time. When I was released, I was still hobbling about on crutches then…"

EXTERIOR: MIDDLE DISTANCE SHOT OF CAR DRIVING THROUGH THE PYRENEES. DAY.

NARRATOR (CONT'D V.O.): "… I heard that Herbert Matthews, of the New York Times, was driving with Sefton Delmar, of the Daily Express, to Paris. I had nothing holding me in Spain. I asked if I could go with them.

I

NTERIOR: CAR DRIVING THROUGH THE PYRENEES. DAY.
DELMAR driving, MATTHEWS in the passenger's seat. ALLAN in
the back seat with his crutch, bandaged leg, and various items of
luggage sharing the back seat.

NARRATOR (CONT'D V.O.): "The drive through the
Pyrenees scared me."

NORMAN (V.O.): "Ted, what happened to Gerda?"

NARRATOR (CONT'D V.O.): "Gerda? Oh... The hospital at
El Escorial. It was growing dark. Someone slapping me awake, I
think. I think. I still held the belt in my hand. It was an English
hospital. I asked if they had seen a woman, a red haired... "Yes.
Gerda Taro. Yes. She's here." They wouldn't let me see her. They
said she'd just had an operation. They said she was all right. Said I
could see her in the morning. They gave me a tetanus shot, put a
mark, a cross on my forehead."

PARTIAL DISSOLVE TO: HOSPITAL WARD, 1937. A very
crowded hospital ward. Many of the wounded lie on stretchers on
the floor of the ward. All the beds are full.

We see faintly, in the background of this partial dissolve, an
image of Ted in the car crossing the Pyrenees, more clearly in the
foreground, TED, on a stretcher on the floor, talking to a NURSE.

Ted: "Will I be able to see her in the morning?"

Nurse: "Yes."

Ted: "How is she?"

The English nurse smiles: "She's all right. She's suffering
from shock but I believe she'll be all right."

Ted: "She needed an operation?"

Nurse: "Naturally. Why do you think we gave her one?"

Ted: "I don't know."

DR.CALDWELL comes over to Ted's cot: "How do you feel?"

Ted: "Good. Fine. Can I see Gerda?"

Dr. Caldwell: "No, I'm afraid not. Not yet. She's suffering from shock. It would be bad for her if you saw her."

"But I might be good for her. I love her. I want to marry her."

"It would not be good for her," Caldwell says, his mouth tightening.

DISSOLVE: back to the car. Ted in the back seat. The NARRATOR (V.O.) tells us that, "The doctor told me that when she had been brought in she had asked to send a cable to Paris, to *Ce Soir* and to Capa. He had done that. My pain had become worse, and he gave me a shot of morphine. "There. Now you'll go to sleep." "Does she say anything?" I asked. "Well, she asked for her camera and I told her I hadn't seen it. When I told her you were here and were all right, she told me to give you her regards."

NARRATOR (CONT'D V.O.): "My watch still showed six-thirty. I asked the time. Three-thirty. I couldn't sleep. I couldn't sleep. Then it was morning. And I think, I think I wanted to give her some of Beth's magic little pills, little trauma pills."

PARTIAL DISSOLVE TO: HOSPITAL WARD: DAWN

NARRATOR (CONT'D V.O.):"At five-thirty Dr. Caldwell came to my stretcher."

CALDWELL: "Well, I think everything looks much better. We just gave her a blood transfusion and she said "Whee, I feel good." She asked about her camera again, and when I told her it was lost she said *"C'est la querre."* She's swell."

TED: "Can I see her now?"

Caldwell: "For God sakes, man, not now. She must sleep now. If she sleeps everything will be all right. You'll see her later."

DISSOLVE: back to the car, LONG VIEW, driving through the French countryside.

NARRATOR (CONT'D V.O.): "I drank some coffee. I was still holding the cloth-woven belt in my hand, fingering the remnants of the fractured wooden buckle. I tried not to think what that might mean. "I'll try and sleep now," I said to myself. "I suppose this is a good story." I think I slept again. Then Dr. Caldwell was walking towards me." Here the narrator's voice breaks up with emotion. "I knew what he was going to tell me."

PARTIAL DISSOLVE TO: HOSPITAL WARD: DAY.

Caldwell: "I'm afraid I have bad news. (pause a beat) Gerda Taro just died."

"Give me a cigarette," says Ted.

Dr. Caldwell lights a cigarette and hands it to Ted. He goes off for a moment and comes back with a hypodermic needle.

Ted protests, "No. I don't need that. For Christ's sake, I don't need it. When I need it, I'll ask for it. I feel no pain."

"You're going to need it," Caldwell says and jabs the needle into Ted's upper arm.

DISSOLVE TO: The car entering the suburbs of Paris.
CUT TO: Ted in the back seat. NARRATOR (V.O.): "I wanted to ask if the doctor was sure Gerda was dead, but I didn't. I wanted to go to sleep and forget. I could not. A nurse came over and told the doctor about another case, and he had to leave. An antiaircraft gun began to fire. The shutters rattled. Caldwell came back. "You'll never know how sorry I am I didn't let you see her. But I didn't know. I really thought she would recover." "Oh, hell. That's all right." "

NARRATOR (CONT'D V.O.): " "If you want," the doctor said, "If you want you can see her now." "Hell, I don't want to see her now." But I did. I didn't believe she was dead.""

DISSOLVE TO: EXTERIOR; PARIS, DAY:

We see Ted, in dark glasses, walking in the streets of Paris, using a pair of crutches. We hear the NARRATOR (CONT'D V.O.): "They brought me upstairs on a stretcher, and I looked at her, and her face was not quite the same. Then they carried me down and I kept slipping on the stretcher, and the boys carrying me told me to hold on or I might fall. They put me in Dr. Caldwell's room. Someone had an English cigarette and gave it to me. I watched the smoke, the smoke curling. Then a nurse brought me Gerda's cigarette case."

DISSOLVE TO: INTERIOR: TED'S PUTNEY APPARTMENT OVERLOOKING THE THAMES. NIGHT. An older TED (the narrator) continues on camera, "There was one cigarette left in the case. I put out the English cigarette and smoked the one in Gerda's case. It was a Spanish cigarette, and I never liked Spanish cigarettes. The doctor asked what I wanted to do with her body and

I wanted to tell him to go to hell, but he meant well, and I asked if he could arrange to get it to Paris. He said he would. Then the nurse came over and said that she was sorry."

Ted sits silently a while. Then continues, "Where was I? ... Ah, in Paris I said goodbye to Delmar and Matthews and registered in a small cheap hotel. I lay in bed most of the time. Days. Days."

DISSOLVE TO: EXTERIOR: PARIS STREET: DAY.

TED with dark glasses and crutches on the Paris street outside the small hotel where he has taken a room.

NARRATOR (CONT'D V.O.): "I called *Ce Soir* to find out where Capa lived. I wanted to see him and tell him I'd tried, I'd tried to take care of Gerda." With emotion: "I couldn't even find her film. I couldn't even save her film."

NARRATOR (CONT'D V.O.): "I left a message at *Ce Soir.* Chim came for me and found me in a hotel room and made me move to Capa's. I didn't want to. "I loved her," I told Chim. "It's all right," Chim said. "Robert knows and still wants you to stay with him." I tried to refuse. "Please, for Robert's sake." I went. Robert Capa greeted me shyly and held my hand and asked about my leg. I was still on crutches."

DISSOLVE TO: INTERIOR: TED'S PUTNEY APPARTMENT: NIGHT TED (older, the narrator): "It was in Robert's flat that I first wrote of Gerda's death. I wrote the story in a fury. Started in the early morning and finished in the afternoon. And when I wrote the story in Paris of course I couldn't say... I had to say it in such a way as to hide the truth from Capa, so that he'd never know she and I had fallen in love and were talking about getting married. She was (pause a beat) falling in love with me, and she kept saying, "I won't fall in love again." "

"And then I forgot about her," Ted says. "I repressed everything personal to do with Gerda and me. A hazy memory. Half a dream. "

Another pause. DISSOLVE TO: Robert's flat in Montparnasse, a large studio loft typical of an artist's studio. Robert's and Gerda's photographs are displayed on one wall. Young Ted and Capa sit facing each other, each smoking, each with a drink in their hands.

NARRATOR (V.O.): "Later I couldn't remember if we had really decided to live together in New York. I could not tell that to Capa. I had to change that."

On camera, in Capa's apartment: Ted to Capa: "I didn't even look after her film for her, and she begged me, she begged me to. I even lost the bloody film!" Ted cries.

NARRATOR (CONT'D V.O.): "Later, in 1954, when I heard that Capa had died, that he stepped on a landmine in Vietman, I thought, "now I don't have to give her to Capa." I got very confused."

SLOW DISSOLVE TO: the Putney apartment, night. Older Ted on camera: "I didn't know who. Give who to Capa? I forgot Gerda for twenty years she disappeared, and then, when I met another redhead, Lucille, who moved and smelled like Gerda, it all came flooding back. Flooding back. But that's another story."

There's a short silence. Then Norman, the author, says (V.O.), "Before we end I want to us to clear up what's true in this story and what's fiction."

Ted says, "Well you invented Gerda sending Beth to China. That's the biggest invention."

"And what do you think about having Gerda send Bethune to China?"

"Hey, I already said, they're going to think its all fiction, some of them. Give them the meat. Let 'em chew."

Norman: "And, did Gerda know Shakespeare?"

"Of course she knew Shakespeare."

"And those were your and her laws of drama?"

"I think so. That's how I remember it."

Norman: "And the moral of the story? of the movie?"

"Till near the end," says Ted, "I thought it was, "Follow your heart, even risking your life for compassion and duty, everything might turn out roses." But the way things panned out I'd say the moral was that fate is feckless, heartless."

"Fate is heartless?" Norman echoes and queries. "What! That's not tolerable."

"Right," says Ted.

"That's why I want to put the homeopathy stuff into your movie. Like an irrelevant "earmark" amendment in a Congressional Bill. I want to talk about the DNA stuff and the harmonics and subharmonics and...".

"Go ahead," says Ted. "It's your movie... "

"But I've got no rationale, no segue. It's just simply and blatantly opportunistic. You were called opportunistic, weren't you, by Bethune and by the Party?"

"I was accused of "adventurism"."

"Oh, like enlisting in the Brigade was adventurism."

"I'll give you a segue," says Ted, "But a limp one. We'll just say the story needs a moral and you decided to use Bethune's maxim, "If it will work, use it." and so you're using this vehicle to bring attention to Benveniste and your homeopathy work."

"That's not quite right. It's the "DNA ultradilution" work. And then even "Bethune's maxim" is a fiction. I don't know if people will be able to handle so many fictions."

"Oh, sure they will," says Ted. "A little juggling, a little truth. A little story telling. And, yes," Ted continued, "we want everyone to read the appendix on the ultradilution."

"Yes, and the sequel. *Norman Allan: the story for Ezra* deals with that too."

"Now that may be pushing the dénouement too far," says Ted, "and we need to keep this simple. So let's end now by quoting Francis, Bethune's wife, her ending to her letter(s) to me."

Soon after he'd finished his Spanish book, *"This Time a Better Earth",* Ted started working on the biography of Norman Bethune, *"The Scalpel, the Sword".*

In 1940, Francis Penney, who had been married to Bethune and divorced, married and divorced twice, and hoped, and hoped to marry him again when he came back from China... Francis came down from Montreal to New York and spent a few days with Ted working on the project. She went home to Montreal with a copy of his, then, very rough draft, and having read it, wrote Ted three letter in response to it. Much of what the world knows about Bethune's personal life comes from those letters. Ah, but I've edited them into one piece. And that's our second appendix. (The explanation of homeopathy is the third appendix. Read it! It is what will save fate from being heartless. The fourth, the last appendix, is the short story, *"My Father in Spain",* which is my, and his, attempt to give a historically accurate account of his trip to Spain. Because this, this is the movie.)

So, in ending her letter of Ted about Bethune, Francis writes...

"You see, I know - we were both gamblers, but our stakes were never small. "Faites vous jeux! Messieurs, faites vous jeux!" cry the Olympians. And the last line: -
"Rien ne va plus"."

The End.

Appendix 1.

Heart of the heartless world,
Dear heart, the thought of you
Is the pain at my side,
The shadow that chills my view.
The wind rises in the evening,
Reminds that autumn is near.
I am afraid to lose you,
I am afraid of my fear.
On the last mile to Huesca,
The last fence for our pride,
Think so kindly, dear, that I
Sense you at my side.
And if bad luck should lay my strength
Into the shallow grave,
Remember all the good you can;
Don't forget my love.

John Cornford

Appendix 2.

Francis Penney's Letter to Ted
http://www.normanallan.com/Misc/Frances.html

Appendix 3.

Beyond substance
http://www.normanallan.com/Sci/bs.html

Appendix 4.

My Father in Spain
http://www.normanallan.com/Lit/stories/TA%20in%20Spain.htm

End Notes: ...

[i] see Appendix 1.

[ii] *This Time a Better Earth* by Ted Allan, University of Ottawa Press, 2015

[iii] *Paris Match* was founded in 1947. But in the movie...

[iv] have to say again that Gerda telling Ted to tell Bethune to go to China is a conceit.

[v] this too is made up, but Hemingway deserves a few fictional slurs.

[vi] Polish born Soviet officer, Karol Waclow Swierczewski, served in the Brigade as General   Walter.

[vii] Ted suffered a crushing injury to his right thigh. He was in hospital for several weeks, used crutches for many, many more weeks, and used the (1930s, 40s, 50s equivalent of) a tensor bandage for the longest time.

Made in the USA
Charleston, SC
10 April 2015